Meet the Cats

Written by Katharine Willard

Illustrated by Rita Ribeiro Lopes

Collins

a rain hat

a light box

a rain hat

a light box

feed the cats

a long tail

feed the cats

a long tail

a pink sheep

a fun fight

a pink sheep

a fun fight

Review: After reading

Use your assessment from hearing the children read to choose any GPCs, words or tricky words that need additional practice.

Read 1: Decoding

- Use grapheme cards to make any words you need to practise. Model reading those words, using teacher-led blending.
- Ask the children to follow as you read the whole book, demonstrating fluency and prosody.

Read 2: Vocabulary

- Look back through the book and discuss the pictures. Encourage the children to talk about details that stand out for them. Use a dialogic talk model to expand on their ideas and recast them in full sentences as naturally as possible.
- Work together to expand vocabulary by naming objects in the pictures that children do not know.
- On page 10, ask: What word tells you something about the toy sheep? (*pink*)

Read 3: Comprehension

- Encourage the children to compare a cat they have seen with those in the story.
  For example, ask: What sort of tail did your cat have? What sort of games did it play?
- Reread pages 2 and 3. Ask the children to describe the box the cats are in. Ask: Is it heavy? (e.g. *no, it is light*) Can the children mime holding a light box and then a heavy box?
- Turn to pages 14 and 15. Ask the children to tell you what happened in the story, using the pictures as prompts. Ask questions, such as: What did the cats arrive in? (e.g. *a box*) What did they do first? (*eat*) What was special about one of the cats? (e.g. *it had a long tail*) How did the cats have fun? (e.g. *by play-fighting*)